Though right now you're little,
it won't be very long

until you grow to be like me . . .
Big and brave and strong.

A world of possibilities
is waiting there for you.
I wonder where you'll go,
I wonder what you'll do . . .

Even when you're scared,
be bold, dream big, stand proud.

Be yourself, be free.
Let your roar be **loud!**

Give new things a try.
Make sure you have some fun!

Life's one big adventure
and it's only just begun.

You really are amazing,
so dream big every day.
I'll be here beside you
to cheer you on your way.

Look up with wonder
at the sky at night.
Just like the moon and stars,
keep shining your own light.

Dare to dream your biggest dreams,
and know that I love you.
For when **you** came along, my love . . .

. . . my biggest dream came true.